FAIRY TALES OF LONG AGO

stories retold by Brenda Apsley and Lesley Scott
illustrations by Gill Guile

DERRYDALE BOOKS
NEW YORK

Contents

This 1987 edition published by Derrydale Books.
Distributed by Crown Publishers, Inc,
225 Park Avenue South, New York, New York 10003.

h g f e d c b a

Little Red Riding Hood

Once, long ago in a land far away, a little girl lived with her mother in a house on the edge of a great forest. The little girl always wore a long red cape with a big hood, and everyone came to know her as Little Red Riding Hood.

One day Little Red Riding Hood's mother packed a basket with lots of good things to eat – pies, cheeses, fruit, and a large cake. "I want you to take this basket of food to your grandmother," she told the little girl. "She hasn't been feeling well, and it may help to cheer her up. And I know she'd like to see you."

"I'd like to see her, too," Little Red Riding Hood replied. "I'll leave right away."

The little girl put on her bright red cloak, pulled the hood over her hair, and set off for her grandmother's cottage, which was on the far side of the great forest.

"Be careful," her mother called as she walked towards the tall trees. "Don't wander from the path."

"I won't," Little Red Riding Hood replied. "Don't worry, I know the way."

8

Little Red Riding Hood followed the winding path through the tall trees until she was in the heart of the forest. It was dark and silent, but she wasn't frightened, for she had followed the path many times before, and knew it well.

The forest birds and animals were her friends, and when they saw Little Red Riding Hood they gathered around her. She sat down to rest against a tree, and stroked the rabbits and the deer. Birds and butterflies fluttered around her.

9

After a few minutes Little Red Riding Hood set off along the forest path again, and she walked on until she came to a clearing in the trees. Wild flowers grew in the clearing, and Little Red Riding Hood stopped to pick some. "Grandmother loves flowers," she said. "A bunch will cheer her up."

Little Red Riding Hood was so busy picking wild flowers that she didn't see a large wolf hiding behind one of the thick tree trunks. He watched the little girl carefully, and licked his lips. "That little girl will make a tasty meal for me," he said, smiling an evil smile. "I wonder where she's going. I'll follow her and see."

Little Red Riding Hood put the bunch of flowers carefully into her basket and walked on through the forest. She hadn't gone very far when she heard a strange noise: *thunk, thunk*! She stopped and listened. There it was again: *thunk, thunk*! What could it be?

Little Red Riding Hood soon found out, for as she turned a bend in the path she saw her friend the woodcutter. He was cutting logs and as his axe hit the wood it made the *thunk, thunk* noises she had heard.

"Hello!" called Little Red Riding Hood. "I heard your axe hitting the wood and wondered what it was. Now I know!"

The woodcutter put down his axe and smiled. "I thought I was alone in the forest today," he said. "Where are you going?"

12

"I'm going to visit my grandmother," Little Red Riding Hood told the woodcutter. "She hasn't been well, and Mother thought some cakes and pies might cheer her up."

"I'm sure they will," said the woodcutter. "Where does your grandmother live?"

"She lives in a cottage on the far side of the forest," the little girl replied. "I still have a long way to walk, so I must hurry."

"Yes," said the woodcutter. "Goodbye."

"Goodbye," said Little Red Riding Hood.

The wicked wolf, who had followed Little Red Riding Hood, was hiding nearby, and listened carefully to the conversation. "So, she's going to visit her old grandmother, is she?" he whispered. "I think I'll pay the grandmother a visit, too!" And with that he hurried off through the trees, for he knew a short-cut to the cottage.

When Little Red Riding Hood was still quite some distance from her grandmother's house, the wolf walked up the path to the front door of the cottage. He knocked softly.

"Who is it?" called Little Red Riding Hood's grandmother. "Who's there?"

"It's me, Little Red Riding Hood," said the wolf in a soft, little-girl sort of voice. "Can I come in?"

"Of course you can," said the old lady, and she opened the door.

What a shock she had when she saw the evil wolf standing there! But before she could shut the door again the wolf pushed her into the house, and locked her in the broom cupboard at the back of the house. Then he picked up a nightgown and a frilly lace bedcap from a chair and smiled his wicked smile. "I think I'll plan a little surprise for the girl," he whispered.

With that the wolf put on the nightgown and the frilly bedcap and jumped into Grandmother's bed. He pulled the sheets up around his chin and switched off the light. "Now all I have to do is wait!" he said.

16

It wasn't long before the wolf heard a quiet knock at the door. "Who is it?" he called in a soft voice that was just like Grandmother's. "Who's there?"

"It's me, Little Red Riding Hood," said the little girl. "Can I come in, Grandmother?"

"Of course," said the wolf. "Come in, my dear. The door isn't locked."

Little Red Riding Hood was surprised to find the room in darkness. "Where are you, Grandmother?" she asked. "I can't see you, it's so dark in here."

"I'm over here – in the bed," the wolf said. "The light hurts my old eyes, so I turned it off. Come closer, my dear, and let me look at you."

Little Red Riding Hood put down her basket and walked across the room to where she could see the shape of the bed. She held out the bunch of wild flowers. "I thought these flowers might cheer you up, Grandmother," she said. "I picked them in the forest."

"Why, that is very kind of you," said the wolf, but as he reached out to take the flowers Little Red Riding Hood gasped and took a step back.

She had seen the wolf's sharp claws, and she was frightened. "Why, Grandmother, what long, sharp nails you have!" she said.

"Yes. Perhaps you could cut them for me later?" said the wolf. "Now, come closer, my dear, and let me look at you."

Little Red Riding Hood moved closer to the bed and looked into the eyes that she thought were her grandmother's. She cried, "Why, Grandmother, what big, bright, black eyes you have!"

"Yes, all the better to see you with, my dear," replied the wolf. "Come closer, my dear."

Little Red Riding Hood took another step towards the bed, then she stopped and stared. One of the wolf's long, furry ears was peeping out under the frill of Grandmother's frilly bed cap!

"Why, Grandmother, what big ears you have!" said Little Red Riding Hood. "They're covered in fur!"

"Yes, all the better to hear you with, my dear," said the wolf, smiling his evil smile.

As he smiled Little Red Riding Hood saw the wolf's long, white, pointed teeth. "Why, Grandmother, what long, sharp teeth you have!" she cried.

At this the wolf threw back the bedclothes and grinned. "All the better to EAT you with, my dear!" he growled, and leaped out of the bed.

When Little Red Riding Hood saw that it was a wolf in the bed, and not her grandmother, she screamed and screamed. "Help! Help!" she cried. "It's a big bad wolf, and he's going to eat me!"

The wolf chased Little Red Riding Hood all around the cottage, but he couldn't catch her, for the frilly nightcap kept falling over his eyes, and he kept tripping over the hem of Grandmother's nightgown.

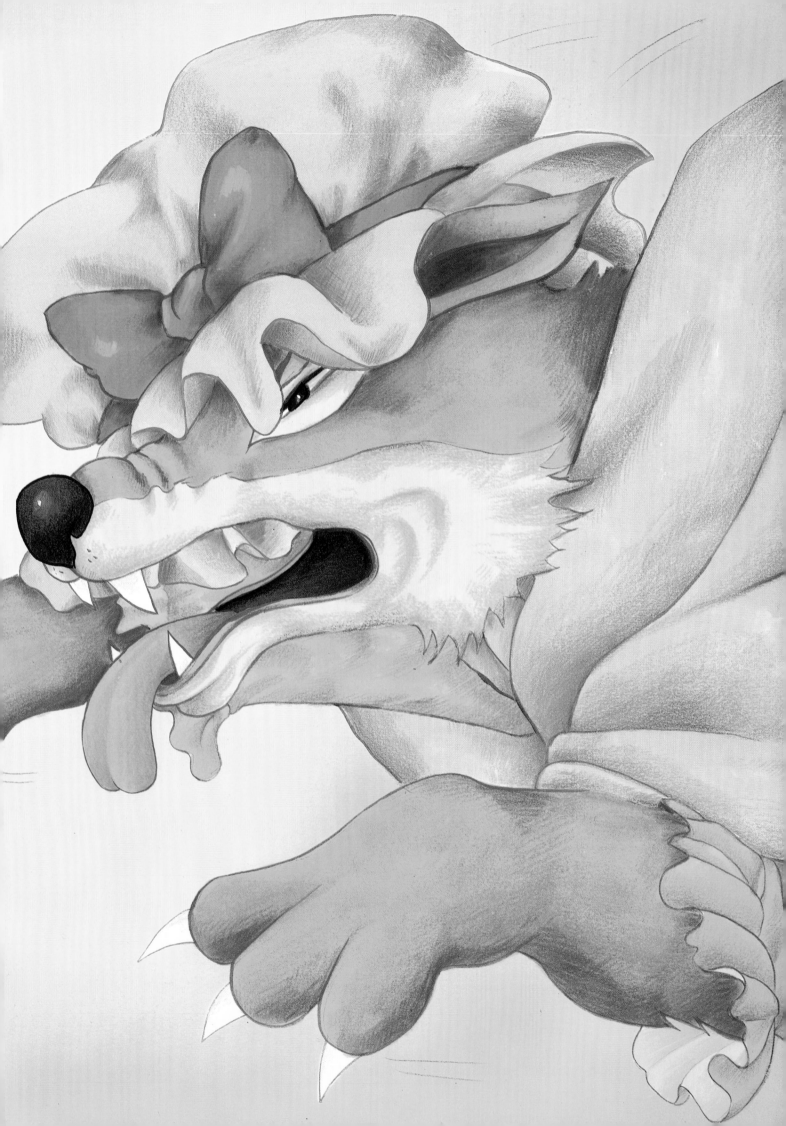

Far off in the forest, the woodcutter heard Little Red Riding Hood's screams, and he ran towards Grandmother's cottage as fast as he could.

When he burst in through the door the wicked wolf took one look at the woodcutter's shiny big axe and rushed out of the door. He ran and ran and ran, and he didn't stop running until he was many miles away.

"Thank you," said Little Red Riding Hood to the woodcutter. "You saved my life. But where is Grandmother? I hope the wolf didn't harm her!"

As she spoke the little girl heard a muffled call from the cupboard at the back of the house. She unlocked the door and found her grandmother frightened and shocked, but unharmed. "Thank goodness you're safe!" she said.

"I'm fine," said Grandmother, "and you're fine, too, thanks to our friend the woodcutter." She turned to him. "What reward can I give you?"

"A piece of the fine cake that Little Red Riding Hood's mother baked would be reward enough," said the woodcutter. And all three of them sat down to enjoy a slice of the cake.

The Little Mermaid

Far, far out to sea, where the ocean is the color of the bluest sapphires and as clear as glass, the water is so deep that no human can imagine its depth. Here, silver shoals of fish dart and play, and here, too, live the people of the sea.

Right at the bottom of the ocean is the sea king's palace. Its walls and roof are made of mother-of-pearl, its windows of the finest shells, and its doors are studded with pearls. Around it are strange gardens, where trees of blue and green, and coral flowers, bloom in the dim sunlight, and the people of the sea play in the caves.

At the time of our story, the sea queen had been dead for many years, and the king lived with his mother, a wise and proud old lady, and his six daughters. They were all very lovely, but the youngest was the loveliest of all. Her eyes were the color of the sea, her hair like gold, and her skin like rose petals. But her loveliest feature was her voice. When she sang, it seemed as though silver bells were gently chiming, and the people of the sea would come from far away to hear her.

Around the palace were gardens, and each of the mermaids had their own little garden, where they would grow the strange plants that grew in the sea. The five elder daughters of the sea king also had in their gardens objects they had found in wrecks on the bottom of the sea – golden cups, and silver dishes studded with gems. But the little mermaid had in her garden the statue of a boy, which she would sit and look at for hours.

She loved to hear tales of the world above the waves,
although she had never seen it herself. When each of
the princesses reached the age of fifteen, the king led
them up to the surface of the water so that they could
see the land for themselves, and when they returned
they would tell their youngest sister all about what
they had seen in the human world. As she grew older,
she longed more and more to see this world for herself,
and would plead with her father to let her accompany
one of her elder sisters to the surface. But every time,
the sea king would say, "You shall go on your fifteenth
birthday, and not before. Your sisters have had to
wait, and so must you."

And then at last it was her fifteenth birthday. There were great celebrations below the sea, with dancing and singing, and then it was time for the youngest mermaid to make her way to the surface of the sea. Her father went with her at first, until they could see the moonlight quite clearly above the surface of the water, but then, knowing how she had longed to see the world for herself, he smiled at her and dived down into the ocean depths once more. The little mermaid rose higher and higher in the water, until finally she reached the surface, and looked about her.

A long way away stretched the land, green and brown, with cliffs of milky white. The moon and stars smiled down upon it as she looked, and then the sound of laughter and song caught her attention.

There was a great ship passing just nearby. Lights blazed aboard it, and fireworks flashed and crackled in the air, dazzling the little mermaid, who had never seen such things before. She gazed, entranced. Music sang out over the water, and cannons roared.

26

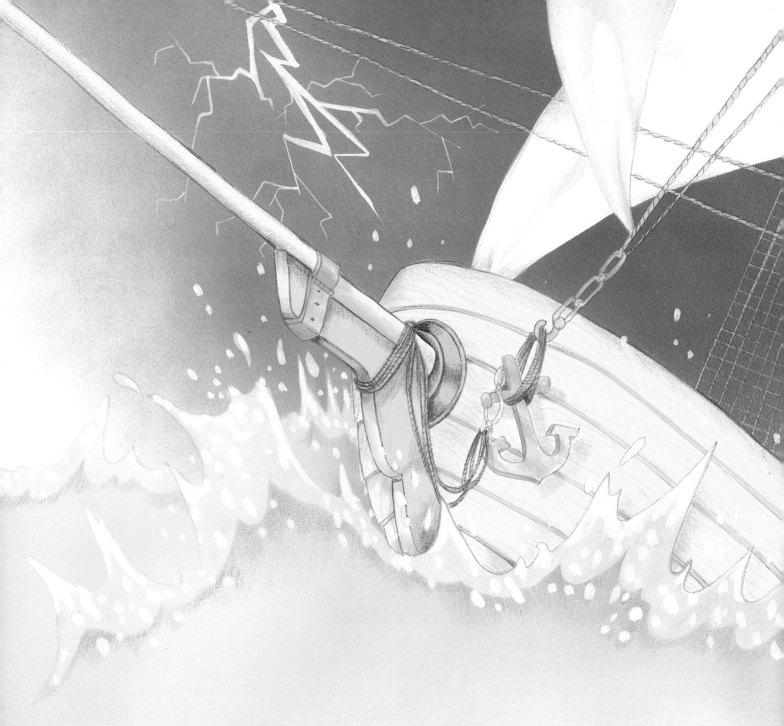

It was the birthday of a prince, and it was being celebrated in great style. Earlier there had been dancing in the royal palace on the shore, but now the prince and his friends could celebrate as they wished. For a long time the mermaid watched them, and one in particular – the young prince himself. Never had she seen anyone so handsome. He looked to her like the statue in her garden beneath the sea, and she could not stop looking at him.

Suddenly, there was a loud peal of thunder from above. The young mermaid was frightened, because she knew what that meant for the ship and its passengers. Then there was another, and a third, and a gale began to blow. The laughter on board ship turned to shouts for help, but it was of no avail as the gale blew the ship about, tearing at its sails, and swelling the sea angrily into huge waves. The mermaid watched in horror as finally an enormous wave buffeted the ship right over in the water, so that those aboard were thrown into the sea, and the ship quickly sank.

The prince had grabbed hold of a piece of the wreckage, and was clinging to it, praying that someone would rescue him. Swiftly the little mermaid swam over to him, to find that he had fainted. She took him gently to the shore, and watched over him on the sand until morning.

As the sun rose, a girl came out of the palace nearby. Quickly, the little mermaid slipped behind a rock and watched. The girl walked for a while by herself, and then, catching sight of the prince on the beach, she rushed down to his side. As she reached him, the prince stirred and opened his eyes.

"You – you have saved me," he whispered.

The little mermaid smiled to herself, for she knew that it had been she who had saved the prince's life, but she did not dare show herself. So she stayed hidden as the girl led the weak prince into the royal palace, and then she slipped back into the sea, and returned home to the palace of the sea king.

"What did you see?" asked her sisters eagerly. "Did you see the sun? And the moon? Were there handsome humans for you to look at? There was a wreck while you were gone – did you see it?"

But the little mermaid would not answer them. She just smiled and said nothing, for her handsome prince was much too precious to be talked about.

Time passed, and the little mermaid spent even more time looking at the statue in her garden, for more than ever it reminded her of the prince. Then one day the longing to return to the surface became too great, and she went to her grandmother and asked for her help.

"I have seen a young prince that I love," she said. "He is human, and – oh, Grandmother, I do so wish to be human too, so that he won't look at me as though I am a strange beast!"

The old queen smiled. "But to any human, that is exactly what you are, my dear. You are half-woman and half-fish. They cannot help it, they regard us as strange because we are different. We have tails instead of legs. And I know of no way that you can have legs. Forget this young prince. He would be far happier to marry one of his own kind."

But the young mermaid could not forget her prince, and as time went on, she grew thin and pale. Then at last her elder sister came to her, and said, "Tell nobody what I am going to tell you. I have heard that the witch who lives in the green cavern has spells that can make anything possible. You could try asking her to help you – but be warned. She asks very high prices for her magic."

The little mermaid did not care how great the price was. Instead, she thanked her sister, and set off at once for the green cavern where the sea witch lived.

The cavern was a long way from the royal palace, and to get there, the little mermaid had to pass through many dangerous places. There were crevices where slimy watersnakes lived, and a deep abyss where the sea disappeared into the heart of the earth. There were whirlpools that could have sucked the little mermaid into their depths, and strange and ugly plants that snatched at her as she went past them.

At last she reached the green cavern where the sea witch lived. She was an old, old woman, even older than the little mermaid's grandmother, and she greeted her visitor with a cackle of laughter.

"Don't bother to explain to me," she said. "I know why you are here. You wish to become human and have legs, so that you can marry your handsome human prince, don't you? Well, I can help you – but the price will be high."

31

"I don't care," said the little mermaid. "The only thing which would make me happy is to become human, and I will give you anything for that."

"You are a fool," said the sea witch. "You will never be happy in the world of humans. Why do you wish to waste yourself on them? But if that is what you want, this is what you must do. I will make up a potion. Go to the surface of the ocean, near the land, and drink the potion as dawn rises. Then you will have legs, and your tail will disappear forever. But you will never be able to become a mermaid again, should you be miserable. And if he should love someone else, you will turn to foam on his wedding day."

The little mermaid nodded. "What is your price?" she asked.

"My price is your voice," said the sea witch. "Your lovely voice. I ask nothing more of you than that. But I warn you, on drinking the potion, you will feel a sharp pain, and from then on, whenever you take a step, it will be as though you are treading on sharp knives. Now, are you still determined to go through with this?"

The little mermaid nodded. The sea witch brewed the potion, and gave it to the little mermaid.

"Remember what I have said," warned the witch. "There is no going back once you have drunk the potion."

The little mermaid nodded again.

Just before dawn, she swam up to the surface of the ocean, close to the shore. Then as the sun came up, she uncorked the potion, and drank it.

At once she felt a great pain, so sharp that she fainted, and lay there unconscious on the beach.

The prince was out riding that morning, and he saw the mermaid on the shore. He rode down to her, and saw that she was very lovely. He lifted her on to his horse, and took her back to the palace.

When she awoke, the little mermaid found herself in a great bed. She sat up and looked around, and realized that she was in the palace she had seen from the ocean. Then she remembered the potion and, looking down, saw that she had legs. She was now human.

She slipped out of bed and stood up. At once she felt a great pain, and remembered what the witch had said. Every time she took a step it was so painful that it seemed as though she were treading on sharp knives. But that did not matter to her as much as the loss of her voice. Now she could never tell the prince that it was she who had saved him from the shipwreck, nor could she let him know that she loved him.

The prince was very fond of the strange young girl he had found on the beach. He took her walking and riding with him, he had her dressed in beautiful clothes, and although she never spoke, he took great pleasure in her company. Then one day, he told her that he was to be married.

"My bride," he said, "is the daughter of a neighboring king. She saved me from a shipwreck, and I love her for that. Are you happy for me?"

The little mermaid's eyes filled with tears, for she knew that everything was for nothing – and she also knew that on the day of the prince's wedding she would be turned into foam on the sea.

But she smiled and nodded, and the prince was pleased.

The day of the prince's wedding came all too soon, and the little mermaid dressed herself in her finest gown for it.

There was a great banquet on the royal flagship after the ceremony, and the little mermaid, the prince's constant companion, was there too. There were fireworks, and singing and dancing on board the great ship, and the prince and his new bride were very kind to the little mermaid, insisting that she sit with them throughout the celebrations.

Then at last, the royal couple retired for the night, and the little mermaid was left alone on deck. She looked out over the waves, and prepared to throw herself into the sea, where she would dissolve and become part of the water. Then, she heard a voice calling her. It was her sister, and she was holding a silver dagger.

"Quick! You haven't much time!" said her sister. "Plunge this dagger into the prince's heart, and you can become a mermaid once more. Hurry!"

The little mermaid took the dagger and lifted the curtain of the prince's bedchamber. But he looked so handsome and kind as he lay there asleep that she could not do it. She ran back to the deck, and hurled the knife far into the sea. Then she plunged into the water after it.

But there was no feeling of dissolving. Instead, she felt herself rising high into the air, and there were others around her, who welcomed her, saying, "We are the spirits of the air! Welcome, you have come to join us!"

The little mermaid looked down, and saw her prince looking for her on the great ship.

"Now I can watch over him for ever," she said, and smiled.

The Ugly Duckling

The mother duck sat on her nest in the bright summer sunshine, wishing that her four eggs would hurry up and hatch. She felt as though she had been sitting there for weeks, waiting for the first tapping sounds that would tell her that her chicks were hatching; and the farmyard pool looked deliciously cool and inviting. She sighed longingly, and settled down again.

The sun grew hotter, and the mother duck soon began to fall into a doze. But suddenly she awoke with a start, and listened hard.

Tap, tap, tap!

Carefully, the mother duck lifted one wing, and looked down at her eggs. One of them had a tiny crack in its shiny blue surface. As she watched, it grew larger, and she could just see the tip of a little beak inside. The eggs had begun to hatch.

Soon, all the eggs had begun to make tapping sounds, and to show little cracks in their shells. All, that is, except one, the largest egg in the nest. That was still silent, and so the mother duck sighed once more, and settled down to await the last duckling's hatching.

It took a long, long time. The other ducklings had hatched out, and were impatient to go to the pond before the last egg began to hatch. Then finally, the mother duck heard the baby bird begin to tap on the inside of the egg, and soon, the shell broke and the last duckling struggled out.

She had to admit that this last duckling was not the prettiest she had ever seen. He was bigger than the others, and instead of having yellow feathers like his brothers and sisters, he was a dirty grey color.

In fact, he was quite ugly. But he would probably grow to be a little prettier.

The mother duck led her ducklings down to the farmyard pond, and took them for their very first swim. They loved it, especially the big, ugly duckling, who swam very well indeed.

"Well, that's one point in his favor, at least," thought the mother duck, thankfully.

41

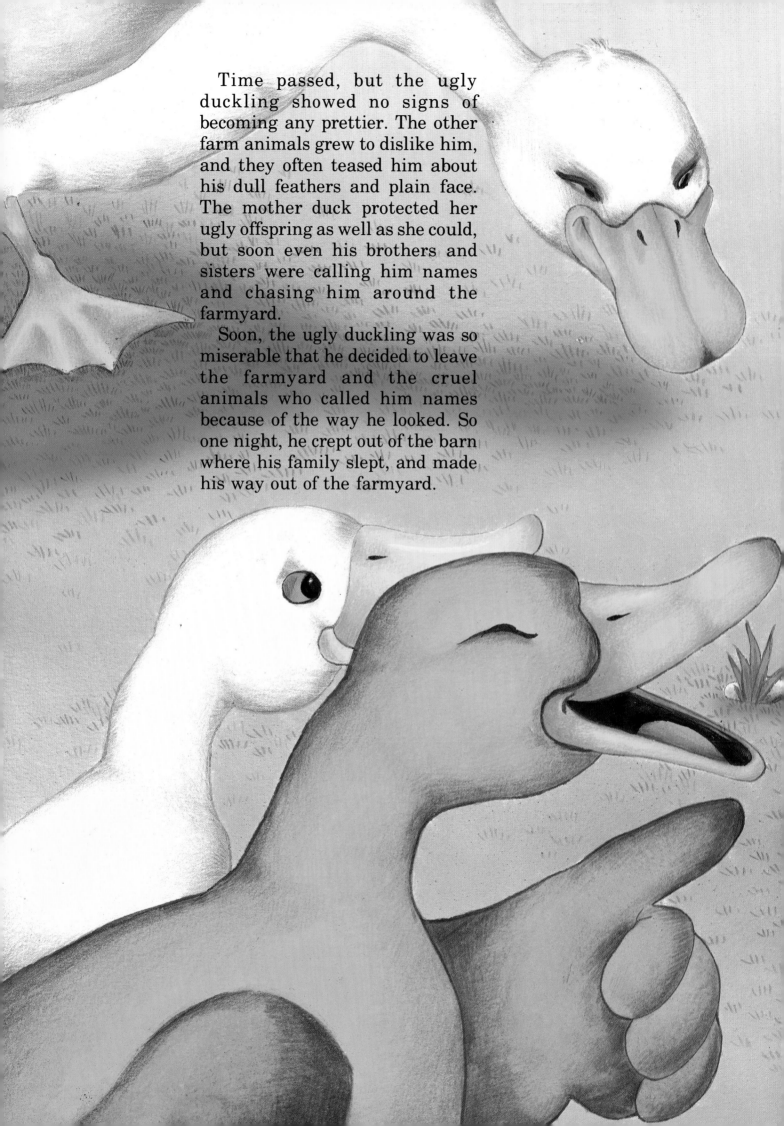

Time passed, but the ugly duckling showed no signs of becoming any prettier. The other farm animals grew to dislike him, and they often teased him about his dull feathers and plain face. The mother duck protected her ugly offspring as well as she could, but soon even his brothers and sisters were calling him names and chasing him around the farmyard.

Soon, the ugly duckling was so miserable that he decided to leave the farmyard and the cruel animals who called him names because of the way he looked. So one night, he crept out of the barn where his family slept, and made his way out of the farmyard.

He waddled along the road for quite a way until he found himself in the middle of the marsh, where wild ducks swam. As soon as they caught sight of him, they gathered round and began to jeer and laugh at him.

"Where do you think you're going, you ugly creature?" they demanded. "Not here with us, that's for sure! Why, you'd frighten away all the grubs we eat, you're so very ugly. Go on, be off with you. Get out of our marsh.!"

The poor duckling bowed his head, and tried to hide in the reeds. He couldn't leave as they said because they were all crowding round.

43

Then suddenly, there was a loud *BANG*! One of the wild ducks gave a squawk and fell forward into the muddy water. At once the others spread their wings and took to the air as quickly as they could, leaving the poor duckling alone with the dead wild duck. There were hunters in the marshes!

The duckling shrank back into the reeds, and watched in horror as the dead duck was picked up by a huge human hand and stuffed into a sack. What sort of place was this that he had come to, where the ducks were shot at by men with big guns? He no longer wanted to stay there. He had to leave the marsh forever.

And so he left the marsh, and walked on further and further, until he was so tired with walking that he couldn't take another step. The duckling sank down onto the ground, exhausted, and wondered what would happen to him.

Quite soon, an old woman came along. She was very short-sighted, and as she caught sight of the duckling on the ground, she thought he would be useful to her.

"Why, this little duck will be able to lay me some eggs," she said to herself. "How nice! Duck eggs for breakfast!"

She picked up the limp and frightened duckling and took him home to her little cottage.

Now the old lady already had two pets, a large ginger tomcat, and a little red hen. They were quite happy by themselves, and were not too pleased at the idea of the duckling coming to share their home. They looked at him, at his dull grey feathers and plain face, and decided that they could have some fun with him.

"Do you know how to purr?" asked the cat lazily, stretching out one paw in the direction of the duckling. The duckling stared at the sharp claws that the cat was flexing, and shook his head in silence.

"Well, then," said the little red hen, who was very proud of herself, "can you lay eggs?"

The duckling looked at her sharp beak, and shook his head again. "I don't think so," he said.

The cat gave a purring sort of laugh. "Then, what can you do?" he asked. "You can't purr and you can't lay eggs. What good are you to the old woman? Or to us, for that matter?"

The duckling shook with fear as the cat and the hen stared hard at him.

"None, I suppose," he said. "I can swim, though."

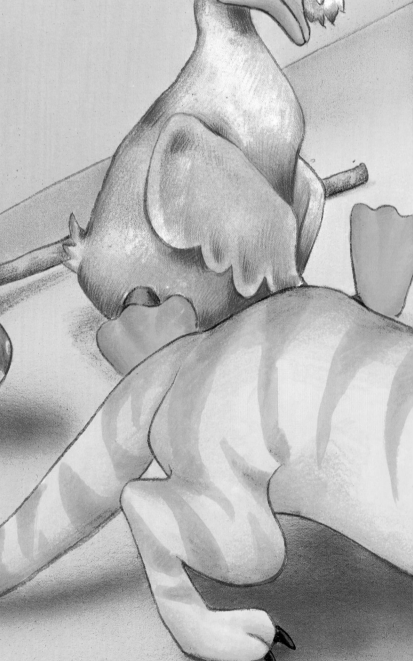

"Swim!" clucked the hen. "He can swim! What a useless occupation."

"Who wants to swim in nasty cold water?" demanded the cat. "What a horrible idea!"

"Oh, no, it's not," said the duckling. "Swimming is lovely. It's the most lovely thing you can imagine!"

"Are you arguing?" demanded the cat, and he stared hard at the duckling. "I say it's horrible, so horrible it is. And if you don't like it here, you can leave."

"As soon as you can," added the hen. "We don't want you here."

47

The poor duckling didn't really want to stay where he was so unhappy either, so later that night he crept out of the cottage and made his way down the road once more.

By now, the weather was turning colder as the autumn came, and the leaves were falling from the trees. The duckling found a stream on which he could practice his swimming, and where there were grubs to eat.

But as the nights grew longer, and the air colder, the grubs began to die off until there was very little food left for the poor duckling.

He made his way downstream until he arrived at a large lake. Swimming on the lake was a flock of wild white birds, more beautiful than any birds the duckling had ever seen before. Their feathers were dazzlingly white, their necks were long and elegant, their heads proud and beautiful. The duckling gazed and gazed at them for a very long time as they swam, and then suddenly, they took to the air and flew away, their long necks stretched out gracefully before them, their strong wings beating the air. The duckling watched them go.

"How beautiful they are," he thought. "It is so unfair. Why was I born so ugly, when there are such beautiful creatures in the world?"

Sadly he continued to swim about the lake.

49

That night, the weather grew even colder. Icy winds blew, and the sky became full of clouds. The water of the lake became very cold, and began to freeze over. The duckling swam even harder, trying to keep warm, but it was no use. The water froze more and more, until the poor duckling had only a very small patch free to swim in.

Finally, by morning, the duckling found that even that patch of water had frozen over. He was trapped in the ice.

He would have died there, if it had not been for two children who lived with their parents quite close to the lake. They had seen from their window that the lake had turned to ice, and had come down to play.

The little girl, whose name was Anne, saw the duckling trapped in the ice. She pointed at him, and her brother, whose name was Peter, ran home to fetch his father. The duckling wondered what would happen now. Maybe they would kill him and eat him, and that would be an end to his troubles. But then he felt the children's father lift him carefully out of the ice, and wrap him gently in a woollen scarf, and he knew that they would not harm him.

The children's father was a farmer, and well used to caring for sick animals and birds. He and the children took the duckling home, and put him before the fire to warm him up. Then they gave him some bread soaked in warm milk. Soon, the duckling began to feel a lot better, and to wish that he could stay in the warm, friendly farmhouse for the rest of his life.

He stayed there all winter, and was looked after by the farmer and his wife, and their two children. The children grew to love him, and they often played games together in the house.

Then the spring came. The duckling could smell the warm weather coming and he longed to go and swim again. He went down to the lake and splashed about in the cool water, enjoying himself very much.

The children laughed to see him so happy, and ran back to the farmhouse to tell their mother. But the farmer's wife was very busy that day, making butter. She had no time to watch the antics of the silly bird, and besides, she wanted the children to come inside and help her with the housework. So Anne and Peter went inside the house, leaving the duckling swimming on the lake.

The smell of spring was very strong in the air, and the duckling suddenly began to feel that he must spread his wings and fly away. He *knew* that he could do it; it was as if something was calling to him. He stretched his neck, spread his wings, and began to fly!

The stream wound on through the countryside for many miles, until it reached another lake, much bigger than the one the duckling had just left.

He circled round over it, looking down, and then his heart gave a great leap. On the shimmering water swam the same magnificent white birds he had seen all those months ago in the autumn. He had to go down and see them once again. They were so beautiful.

53

Down, down, down he flew, until he reached the lake. He folded his wings as he landed on the surface, and swam timidly towards the white birds. They would be sure to chase him away because he was so ugly, he knew that, but he wanted to see them. To his surprise, they came and swam close to him, not sneeringly, but in a friendly way. They dipped their graceful heads to him in greeting, and shyly the duckling did the same. As he did so, he caught sight of his reflection in the clear water of the lake. He stared.

He moved his head from side to side so that there could be no mistake – and there was not. Looking back at him from the water was another of the beautiful white birds, with a long, elegant neck and a small, proud head. Its feathers were as white as the snow that had fallen during the winter. He was a swan!

The duckling raised his head proudly and joined the other wild swans as they swam together on the lake. For the first time, he knew what it was like to belong to somebody, and now he was happy at last. He was no longer the ugly duckling, but a beautiful, proud swan!

The Sleeping Beauty

Once, long ago, the king and queen of a faraway country had a little daughter. They were delighted, because she was their only child, and they had longed for a baby. Plans were made for the little princess's christening, and invitations were sent far and wide. The fairies from the woods and the sea and the air were all invited – except one. She was very old indeed, and nobody had seen her for years because she never left her castle. In fact, some people even thought she was dead! She was furious at being left out, and swore that she would take revenge for this insult.

At last, the day of the christening arrived, and everyone who had received an invitation came to the palace. There were marvelous festivities, singing and dancing, and then came the moment that the king and queen had been waiting for – the fairies who had come to the ceremony each gave the little princess a gift.

These were not ordinary gifts. They were gifts like beauty, gentleness, a sweet singing voice, and many others. One by one, the fairies bent over the golden cradle and gave the baby their gifts, while the king and queen stood by happily.

Suddenly, there was a clap of thunder from outside, and the great doors flew open, bringing a gust of wind into the chamber so strong that people had to cling to each other. Then as it died down, a shape began to appear. It was old and shriveled, dressed in dusty black robes, and carrying a bent and gnarled old stick. It was the old fairy that nobody had thought to invite! And she was very angry indeed.

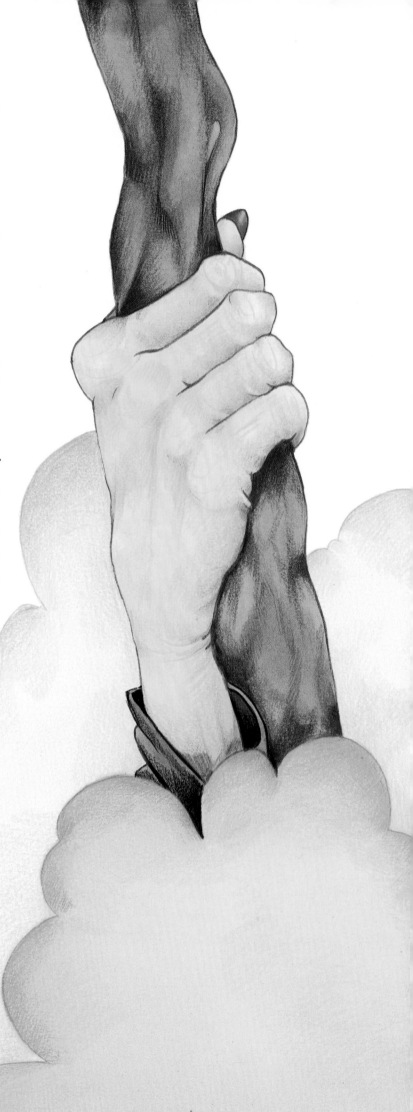

The king and queen at once went forward to her, and tried to offer her their apologies for not having invited her, but she brushed them to one side, and hobbled over to the cradle. The little princess looked up at the old fairy, and began to cry.

"You may well weep!" said the old fairy. "For this insult to me, you will suffer! You may well have all the gifts that these fairies have given you, but I shall give you another sort. At the age of sixteen you will prick your finger upon a spindle, and die!"

The king and queen were horrified, and tried to reason with the fairy, but she merely laughed in their faces. Then, picking up her dusty robes, she began to spin faster and faster and faster, until she was nothing but a blurred shape, and then even that vanished.

In the middle of all the horror, a gentle voice spoke. It was one of the woodland fairies, who had not yet given the princess her gift.

"Don't distress yourselves so much," she said. "I have the power to do something about this evil spell. I cannot remove it altogether, but I can help. My gift is this – the princess will not die when she pricks her finger, but instead will sleep for a hundred years, and wake just the same as when she fell asleep."

The king and queen were grateful to the fairy, but they were still very upset, and the king issued a command that all spindles in the kingdom were to be burned, and nobody was to use one ever again.

The princess grew up, and became a very beautiful and kind young girl. Everyone loved her, and her parents began to forget about the evil spell that the fairy had cast at her christening. But the bad fairy did not forget.

One day, when the princess was sixteen years old, she grew bored with her painting, and decided to explore those parts of the palace that she had never been in before. So she made her way to the small, narrow passages behind the great hall, and up a steep, winding staircase until she reached a series of little rooms at the top. From one of them there came the strange humming sound of someone spinning. The princess had never seen anyone spinning before, and she was very curious. So, gently, she pushed open the door and went inside.

In the room sat a little old lady, wearing a dusty black dress and a white lace cap. In front of her was a spinning wheel, with a spindle on the top.

"Come in, come in, my pretty one," said the old lady kindly, as she saw the young girl. "Have you come to watch me spin?"

"Yes, please," said the young princess, and she sat down on a low stool at the old lady's side. She was so interested in the spinning wheel that at last she asked if she might try it herself.

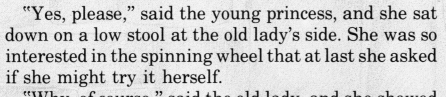

"Yes, please," said the young princess, and she sat down on a low stool at the old lady's side. She was so interested in the spinning wheel that at last she asked if she might try it herself.

"Why, of course," said the old lady, and she showed the princess how to guide the wool on to the wheel from the spindle.

"We'll need to add some more wool," said the old lady. "Would you pass me the spindle, please, my dear?"

The princess reached out for the spindle, but as she did so, she pricked her finger on it, and a drop of blood welled up.

"Ha!" cried the old lady, and in a flash the princess recognized the old fairy who had made her cry when she was a baby. But it was too late. She began to yawn, and to feel sleepy, and had only time to stumble back to her own room before she fell fast asleep.

"The spell is fulfilled!" cackled the old fairy, and she vanished with a peal of laughter.

The prince went on through the palace, finding more and more people asleep, never a soul awake. He went upstairs, and found the passages and corridors littered with sleeping people. They were in every bedroom.

Finally, he arrived at a door with a golden crown painted on it. He turned the handle, and pushed open the door.

Inside there was a beautiful bed, draped in blue silk and lace, and covered with a delicate canopy. On the bed, fast asleep, lay a girl. The prince went over to her side and looked down at her. She was very beautiful indeed, the most lovely girl he had ever seen. Her hair was like spun gold, her skin like velvet, and her mouth was soft and red.

The prince looked at her for a long time. Perhaps this was the beautiful girl the old shepherd had been talking about. He could not imagine there to be one more beautiful in the whole palace. He could hardly take his eyes from her.

"I don't suppose she would mind if I kissed her," thought the prince. "She won't know I did anyway."

And he bent over the sleeping princess, and very softly kissed her mouth.

As he stood up again, he saw with amazement that the princess was starting to wake up. She smiled gently, and then she opened her eyes and looked at him. At that moment, there was a flash, and the good fairy appeared in the room with the prince and princess. She smiled.

"You have broken the spell," she said to the prince. "I give you both my blessing."

The princess sat up, and the prince led her out of the bedroom and downstairs. They passed the servants and courtiers, all of whom were waking up and looking about them. They bowed low when they saw the prince and princess. All over the palace the people were waking up, and by the time the two reached the great hall, the king and queen, with the good fairy by their side, were waiting to receive them.

"Thank you," said the king. "You have broken an evil spell that was laid upon our daughter at her christening. What can I give you to thank you properly?"

The prince looked at the princess, and she smiled at him. "The hand of your daughter in marriage, Your Majesty," he said.

And so it was. The prince and the sleeping beauty were married soon afterwards, and all the fairies of the kingdom were invited to the wedding. The wicked fairy was also invited this time, but she had died many years before, and could no longer make mischief.

When the time came, the prince and princess became king and queen, and ruled their country wisely and well.